Harriet Ziefert

Grandma's Wedding Album

paintings by

Karla Gudeon

Blue Apple Books

For my five grandchildren, all of them Zieferts—Will, Nate, Sylvie, Charlie, and Lucy

— H.M.Z.

For my favorite husband

— K.G.

Published in the United States 2011 by
Blue Apple Books, 515 Valley Street, Maplewood, NJ 07040
www.blueapplebooks.com
First Edition 03/11 Printed in China
ISBN: 978-1-60905-058-0

2 4 6 8 10 9 7 5 3 1

"I'll be the bride. And you be the groom," said Emily to her brother, Michael.

"Okay," said Michael.
"Then let's show Grandma how we look."

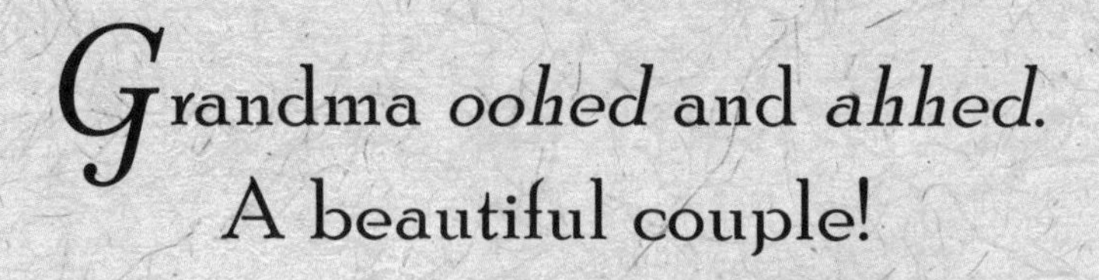

Grandma *oohed* and *ahhed.*
A beautiful couple!

Then she asked,
"Would you like to see the REAL bride and groom?"

"I'd like to see you as a bride," said Emily.
"And Poppy as a groom," said Michael.

So Grandma took out her wedding album
and began the story
of how she met Poppy.

"We met at a picnic
in the park.
As soon as we were
introduced, I knew Poppy
was the man for me,"
said Grandma.

"Poppy said he knew
we were meant to be."

"We dated
for a whole year.
Then Poppy asked me
to marry him.

Here we are telling
the news to my parents—
your great-grandparents,
Nina and Joe."

"This is the wedding invitation we sent to family and friends," said Grandma.

"How many people did you invite?" asked Michael.

"We had more than one hundred guests. They came from all over."

"When the
wedding day arrived,
Poppy felt like a king.
And my friends made
me feel just like
a queen."

"The wedding took place
in a boathouse
near a beautiful lake."

Grandma continued,
"The wedding party posed
for pictures just before
the ceremony."

"Down the aisle
came the ring bearer.
He carried two gold rings:
one for me
and one for Poppy,"
said Grandma.

"He knew his job was
to keep the rings safe."

"Then came the flower girl."

"What does a flower girl do?" asked Emily.

"Her job is to spread petals on the ground so the bride has a beautiful path to walk on."

"The musicians played
'Here Comes the Bride.'

It was my turn to proceed
down the aisle.

I was happy. I was scared.

But when I saw Poppy smile,
all my fears vanished."

"I still remember our vows:

I vow to bring you happiness, and I will treasure you as my companion. I promise to be your wife and your best friend."

"Is Poppy really your best friend?" asked Emily.

"Yes, he is," said Grandma.

"There was a fancy party
in the boathouse with lots
of food and jazzy music.

Here we are dancing
our first waltz."

"Poppy and I gave each
other a piece
of the wedding cake.
It was delicious!

Then I threw my bouquet.
My best friend Ruth
caught it, and she married
one year later."

"Friends and family
wished us well,
and we left
on our honeymoon.

We got in the car and
drove to a beautiful resort
in the mountains."

JUST MARRIED

Grandma ended with, "Some day, when you're grown-ups, you'll have your own weddings."

"And I hope I'll be there to celebrate and dance, all night long!"

Wedding Traditions

Weddings are joyous occasions when two people honor and celebrate their love and commitment to each other. Given America's cultural mosaic, traditions from countries and cultures around the world have become fixtures in our present-day weddings. From jumping the broom to painting the bride's hands with henna; from *something old, something new, something borrowed, something blue* to creating new rituals to be passed down to future generations, traditions make each wedding unique and memorable for family, friends, and the newlyweds.

African-American

Jumping the Broom, an African tradition brought to America by the slaves of the South, was created since slaves could not legally marry. The bride and groom enter into a new life by 'sweeping away' their former single lives, then jumping over the broom (or an imaginary line) to begin their new adventure together.

The *ankh* is the African symbol for eternal life, love, and unity and can be used on African wedding invitations and decorations.

Scottish

Kilts are often worn by the groom and his best man.

During the ceremony, the groom welcomes the bride to his family by wrapping her in his family's tartan sash.

Bagpipes are often played at Scottish weddings.

French

The newly married couple drink a toast from a two-handled cup—*une coupe de mariage*—at their reception.

Hawaiian

Leis (which symbolize love and respect) are usually part of the wedding, and the ceremony begins with the bride and groom exchanging these flower garlands.

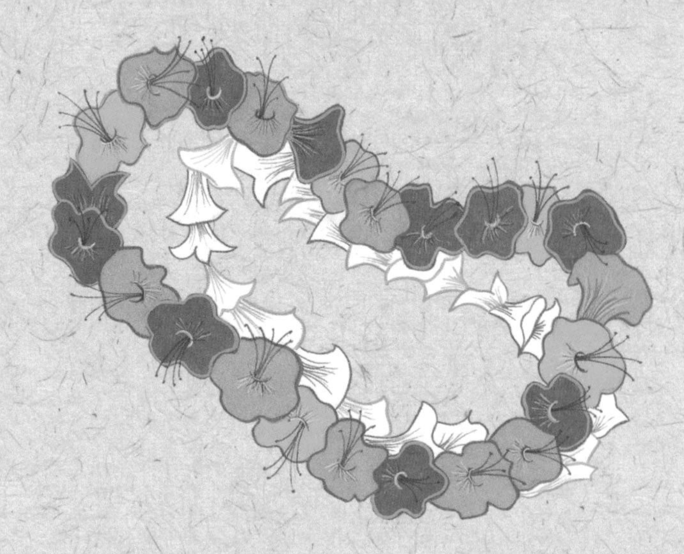

Brides often wear strands of pink and white *pikake*, or headpieces made with *haku* flowers.

Native American

In the Navajo tradition, the bride's dress has four colors, each representing one of the four directions: black for north, blue for south, orange for west, white for east. The couple faces east (the direction of the sunrise) during the ceremony to symbolize their new life together.

Irish

Handfasting is an ancient Celtic wedding ritual in which the bride's and groom's hands are tied together.

An Irish bride's wedding ring is called a *Claddagh* ring: two hands holding a heart topped by a crown. The heart signifies love, the hands faith, and the crown honor.

"Let love and friendship reign" is the ring's motto.

Greek

The pinning of money on the bride's dress is a well-known tradition. Sometimes guests dance with both bride and groom and pin money on their clothes.

Kalamatianos is a Greek line dance, which can be performed at weddings and is led by a person holding one end of a handkerchief.

Philippines

The bride's veil is pinned to the groom's shoulder, signifying that the couple is now clothed as one.

The traditional dance is the *pandango* and is often danced for hours.

Italian

In Italian weddings, 'something blue' is replaced with 'something green.' According to tradition, green brings good luck to the couple.

Confetti—sugar-coated almonds—are served to symbolize both the bitterness and the sweetness of life.

Japanese

In a Japanese wedding banquet, foods are served that symbolize wishes and hopes for happiness, prosperity, long life, or many children. For instance, clams are served with both shells together, symbolizing the new couple.

Sometimes, 1,001 origami cranes (symbols of longevity and prosperity) are folded to bring luck, good fortune, fidelity, and peace to the newlyweds.

Jewish

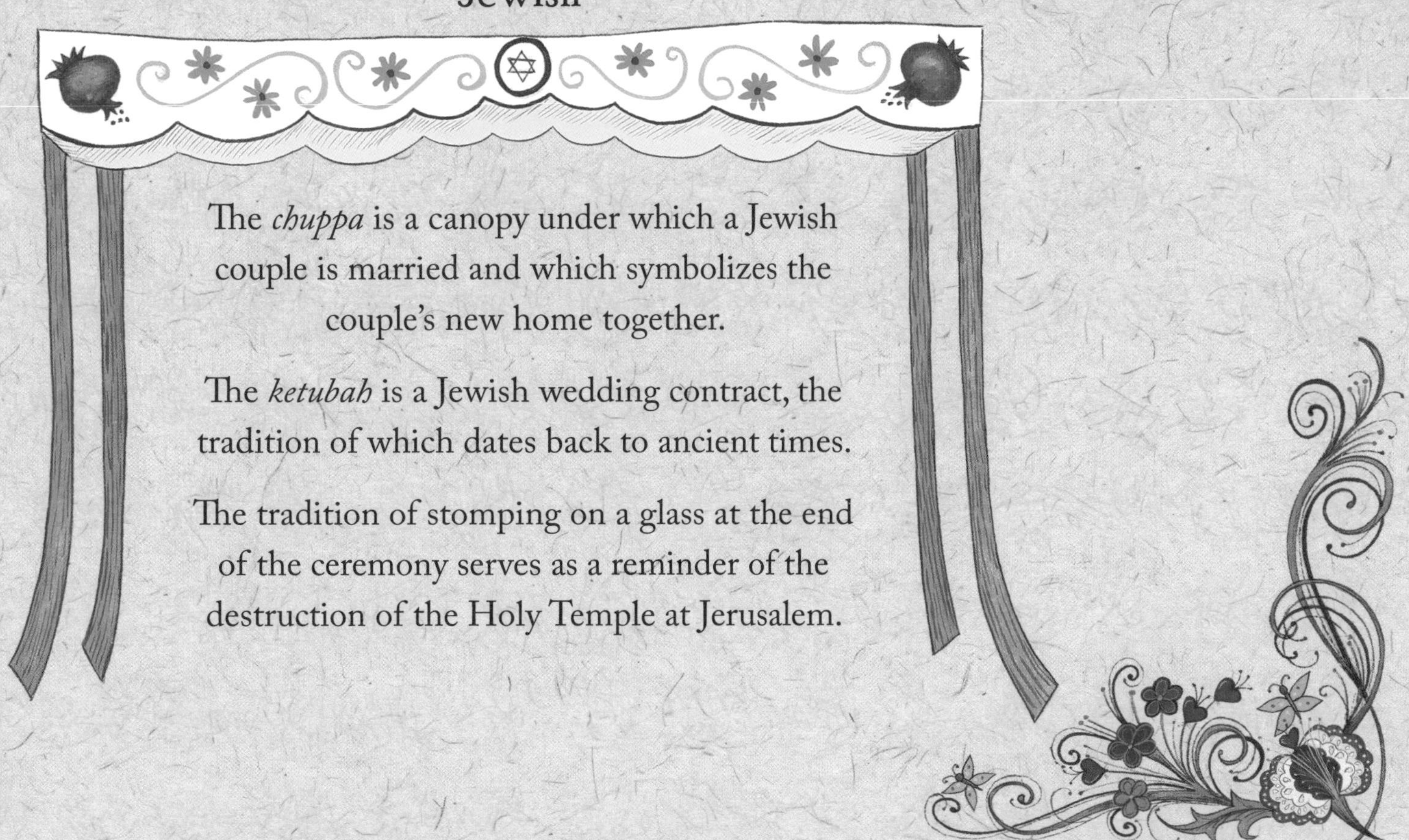

The *chuppa* is a canopy under which a Jewish couple is married and which symbolizes the couple's new home together.

The *ketubah* is a Jewish wedding contract, the tradition of which dates back to ancient times.

The tradition of stomping on a glass at the end of the ceremony serves as a reminder of the destruction of the Holy Temple at Jerusalem.

Korean

Traditionally, the groom gave a wild goose (symbolizing faithfulness, as a goose mates with one partner for life) to his new mother-in-law as a sign of his faithfulness to her daughter. Today, Korean families use a *kirogi*, a wooden goose.

Three red circles, *yonji konji* (originated hundreds of years ago to ward off evil spirits), are painted on the bride's cheeks.

The wedding banquet is called *kook soo sang* (noodle banquet). Buckwheat noodles are among the entrees, symbolizing the couple's long life together.

Polish

At the reception, the bride's and groom's parents bring the couple bread (sprinkled with salt) and a goblet of wine. Bread symbolizes the hope that their children will never be hungry; salt, that they must learn to deal with the difficulties of life; and wine, the hope that the newlyweds will have good health and good cheer.

Chinese

The color red symbolizes love, joy, and prosperity. The bride's wedding gown, invitations, candles, and wedding gift boxes are often red.

Weddings are usually held during the Chinese New Year, which welcomes and celebrates the coming of spring.

The Chinese symbol for double happiness is used during the wedding festivities.

Scandinavian

For luck and prosperity, the Swedish bride's father puts a silver coin into his daughter's left shoe; her mother puts a gold coin in the right shoe.

Kransekage, a Scandinavian cake, is served at weddings. Made of different sizes of ring cakes, the rings are stacked one on top of the other, largest at the bottom, smallest at the top.

Thai

The bride's and groom's mothers walk to the altar and put *puang malai* (flower garlands) around the couple's shoulders to wish them good luck.

Puerto Rican

Capia (ribbon corsages) are pinned on the dress of a bridal doll. At the reception, the bride takes the capia from the doll and pins one on each of the guests.

Mexican

After the vows, a *lazo* (a white ribbon or rosary sometimes made of beads and pearls) is placed in a figure-eight pattern around the groom's neck and then the bride's. It represents the couple's commitment and eternal union.

Arras are thirteen gold coins given from the groom to the bride. They symbolize his commitment to support his new wife and are blessed by the priest during the ceremony.

Ukranian

Korovai, a traditional wedding bread, is served. The bread is round and encircled by a braid of dough. To wish the couple good luck, the bread is decorated with flags, figures, birds, and the tree of life.

Hindu

During the wedding days, there is a *tilak* ceremony (when the groom is anointed on his forehead) and a ceremony for adorning the bride with henna (called *mehndi*). The color of *mehndi* signifies the essence of love in a marriage and is put on the bride's hands and feet.

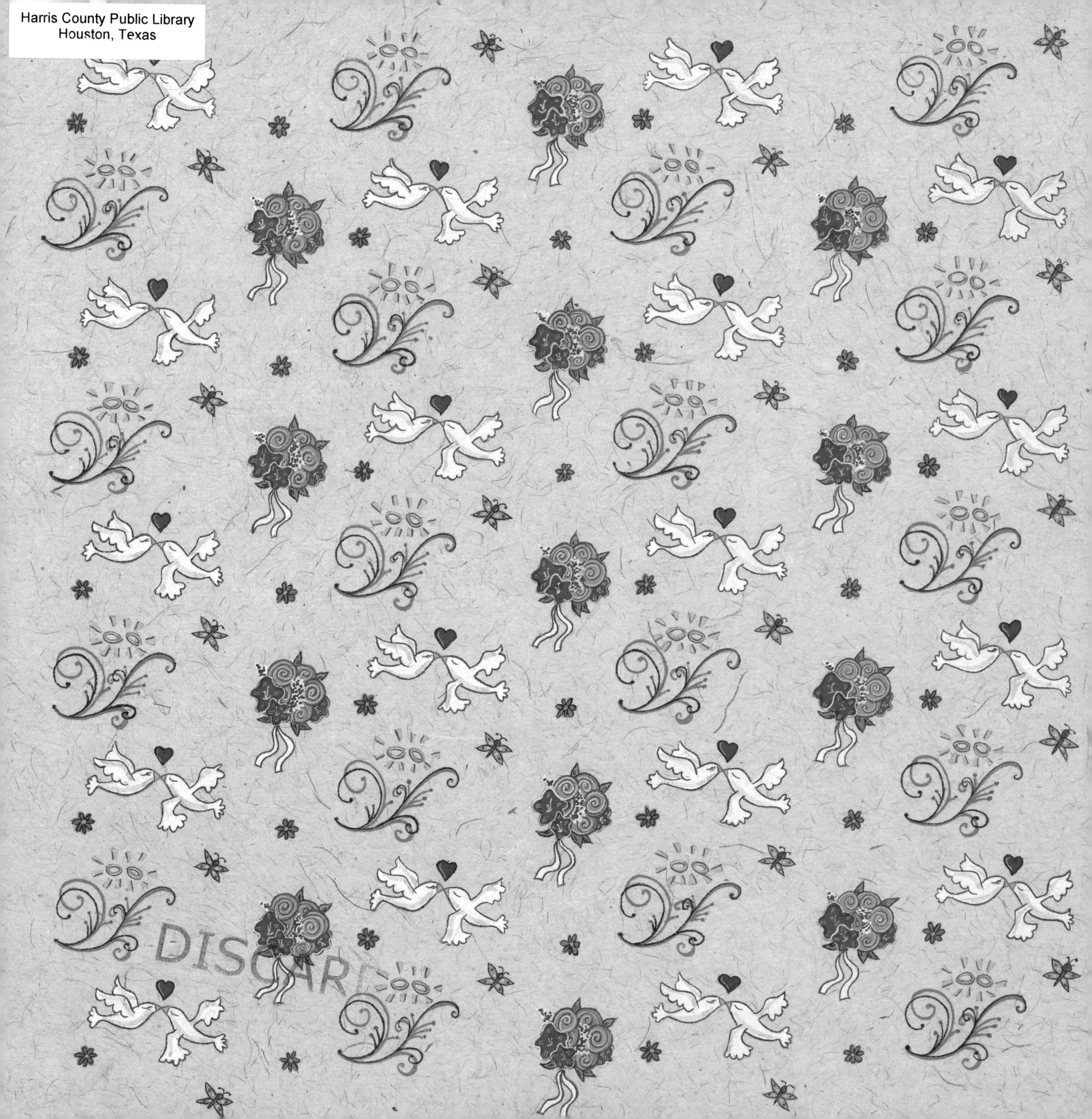